For Emily and Robin M.B.
For Leo N.S.

First published in 2014 by
Hodder Children's Books

Text copyright © Mara Bergman 2014
Illustration copyright © Nicola Slater 2014

Hodder Children's Books
338 Euston Road, London NW1 3BH

Hodder Children's Books Australia
Level 17/207 Kent Street, Sydney, NSW 2000

The right of Mara Bergman to be identified
as the author and Nicola Slater as the
illustrator of this Work has been asserted
by them in accordance with the Copyright,
Designs and Patents Act 1988.

A catalogue record of this book is available
from the British Library.

ISBN: 978 1 444 91419 1
10 9 8 7 6 5 4 3 2 1

Printed in China

Hodder Children's Books is a
division of Hachette Children's Books.
An Hachette UK Company

www.hachette.co.uk

Best Friends

Mara Bergman   Nicola Slater

Hodder
Children's
Books

A division of Hachette Children's Books

D exter McFadden McSimmons McClean,
the dog with the longest legs anyone's seen,
was chasing a ball as fast as he could,
over the bridge and into the wood.

Meanwhile…

Daisy the dachshund was strolling along, humming and whistling to her favourite song.

She ignored the dark

FLASH

as it shot through the wood

and followed her ball just as fast as she could.

Meanwhile...

Lily had been for a wash and a cut
when she went to the park for a walk and a strut.

She too was chasing
her favourite ball,
ignoring the other dogs,
big ones and small.

Three dogs were running. Where would they go?

and **Daisy SO** slow,

Dexter like lightning

and **Lily**, who hated to dirty her claws,

ran ever so lightly
on tippy-toe paws.

Meanwhile...

William was running as fast as he could, calling for **Dexter**, who ran through the wood,

while…

Jack was happily strolling along, looking for **Daisy** and singing a song,

and…

Maddie was searching
and searching for Lily,
who'd just had her hair cut
and looked rather silly!

"Dexter!"
called William,

then Jack,
"Daisy, here!"

Maddie
called, *"Lily!"*

But did they appear?

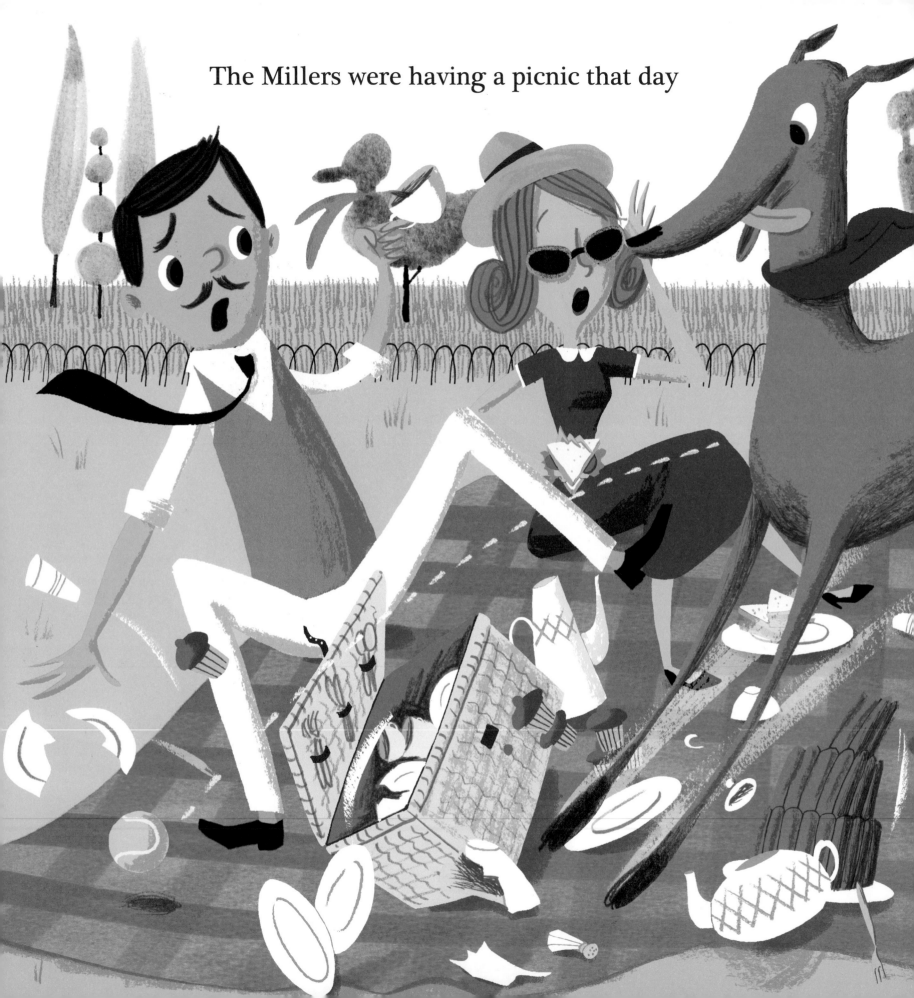

The Millers were having a picnic that day

and **jumped up**
as Dexter
came charging their way,

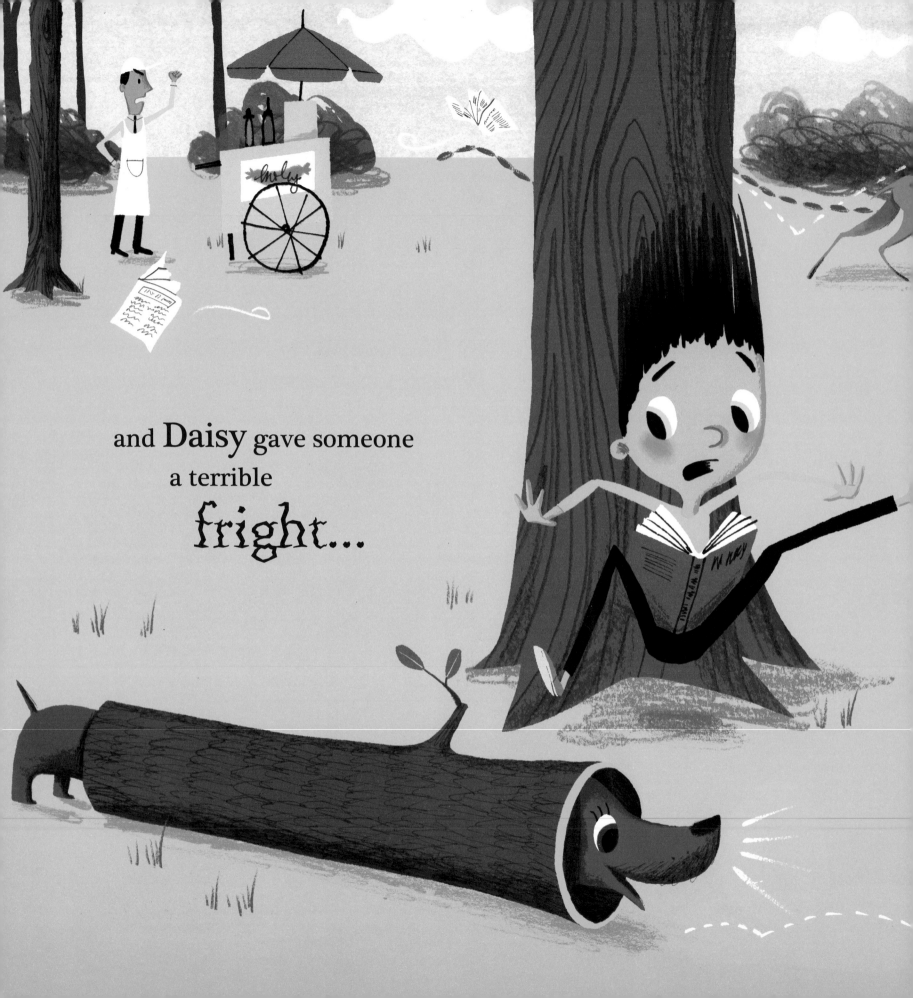

and **Daisy** gave someone
a terrible
fright...

while **Lily** got mixed up
with somebody's kite.

Sandwiches, newspapers, blankets went flying,

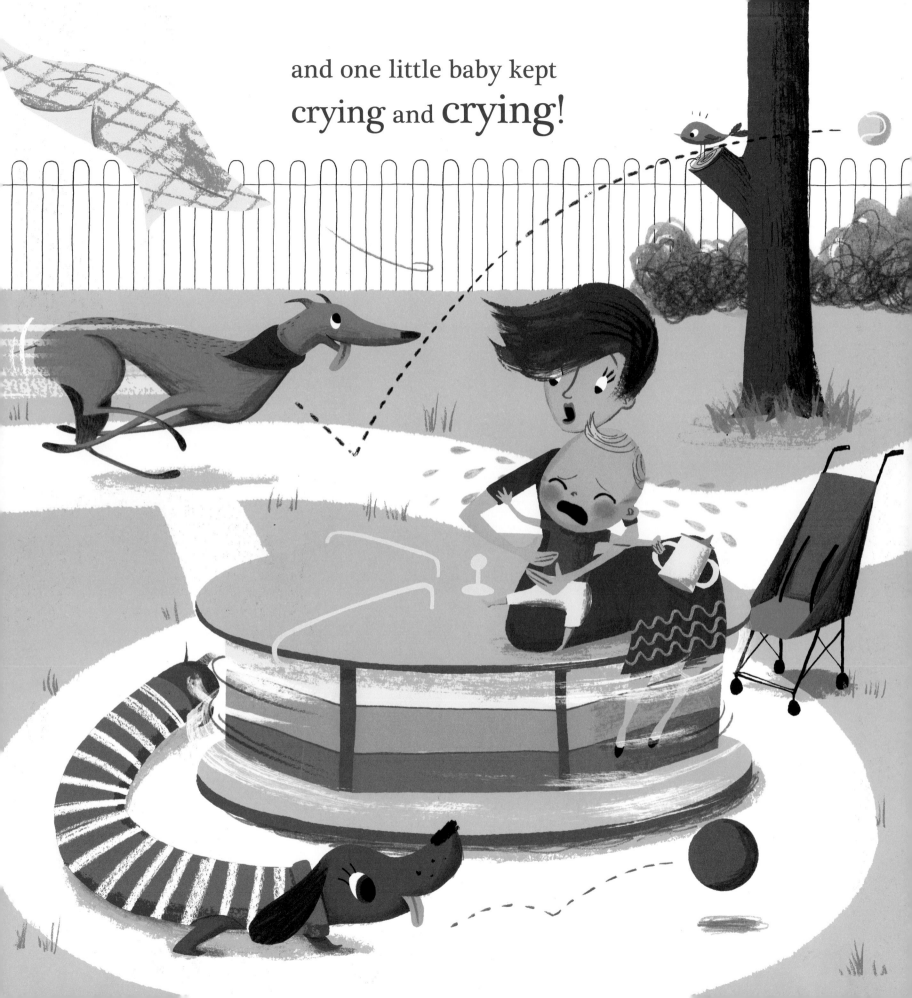

and one little baby kept
crying and **CRYING!**

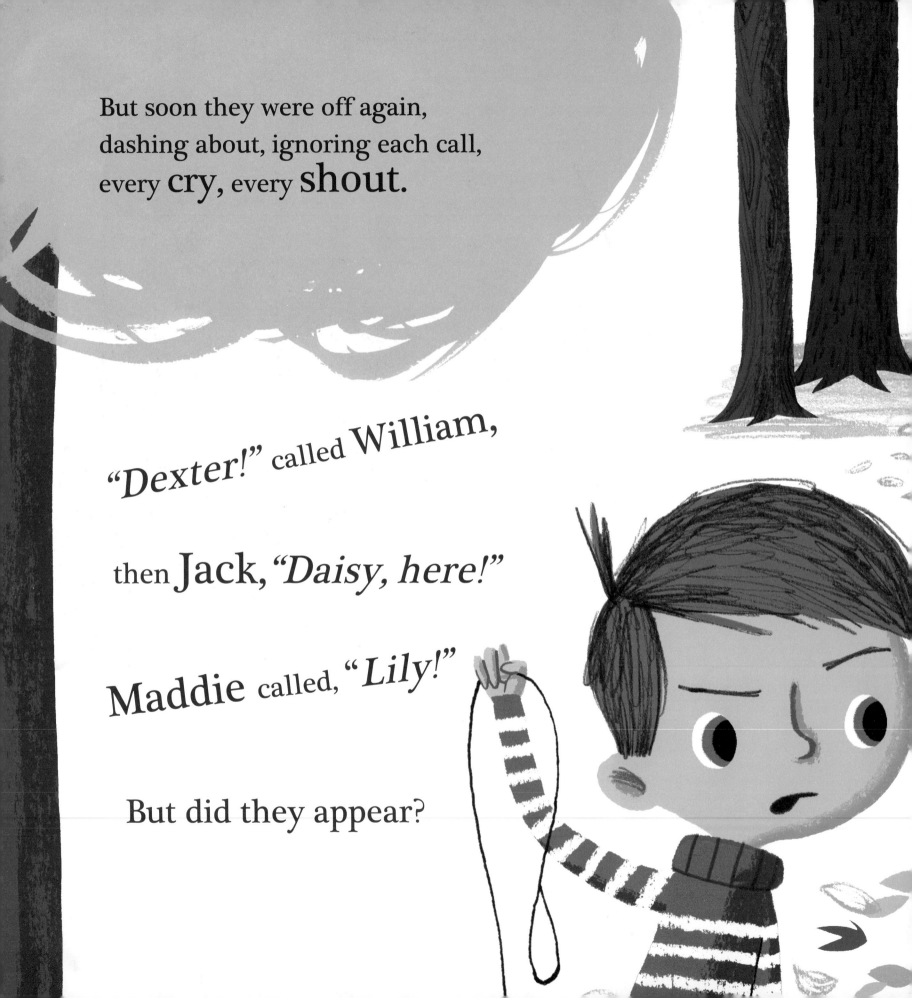

But soon they were off again,
dashing about, ignoring each call,
every cry, every shout.

"*Dexter!*" called William,

then Jack, "*Daisy, here!*"

Maddie called, "*Lily!*"

But did they appear?

THEN…

the children grew worried. What was that sound?
They ran to the stream...

SPLISH!

SPLASH!

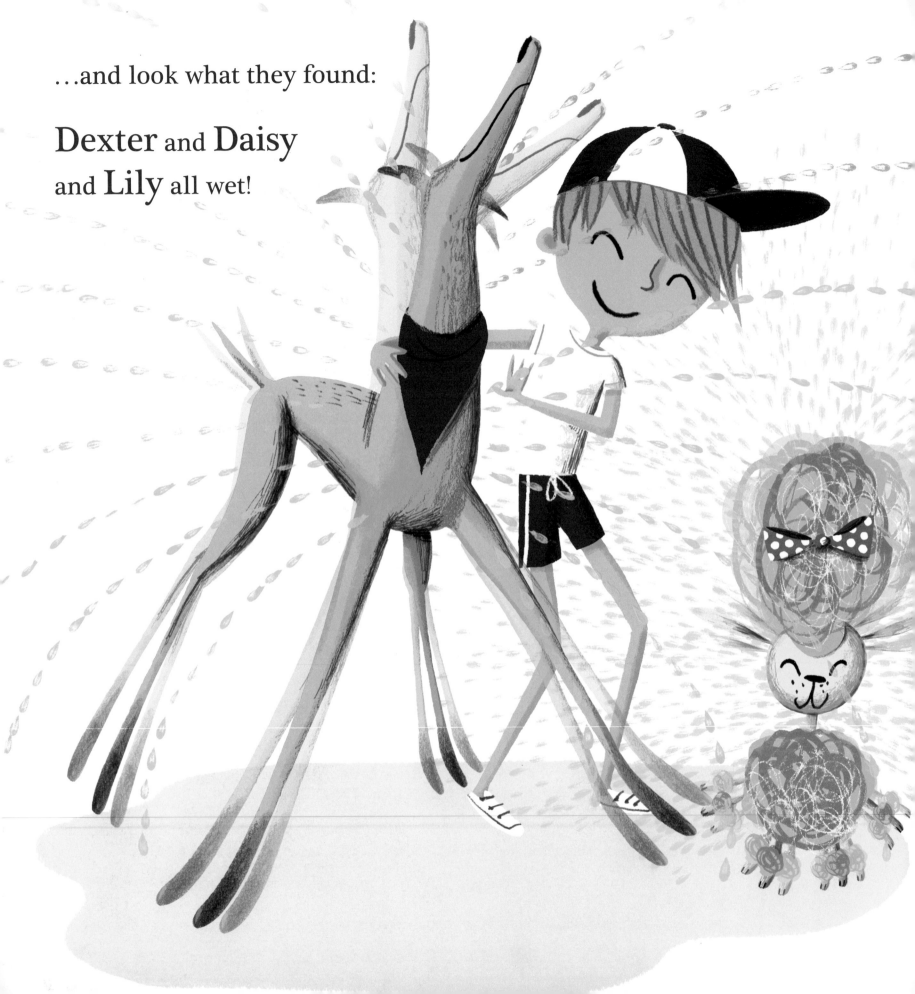

...and look what they found:

Dexter and Daisy
and Lily all wet!

Each was the soggiest, happiest pet.
With a **wriggle** and **shake,** the dogs made a splatter.
The children got soaked, but it didn't matter!

And this is the way that our story ends –
the children and dogs became…

best friends!